The Tomten and the Fox

ADAPTED BY ASTRID LINDGREN

FROM A POEM BY KARL-ERIK FORSSLUND

ILLUSTRATED BY HARALD WIBERG

# The Tomten and the Fox

COWARD-McCANN, INC. NEW YORK

The fox lives in the middle of the forest.

When evening comes he leaves his den.

Where can a hungry fox find something to eat?

He knows.

*Creep silently, Reynard, creep silently to the farm where people live.*

Harald Wiberg

But how light it is!

The snow is so white and the stars so bright.

*Creep carefully, Reynard, creep so that no one can see you.*

Who will see him? There is a light in the window,
and there are people inside the house,
but no one will look out to see a hungry fox
coming through the snow.


*But someone can see you, Reynard,*
*the Tomten who watches the farm at night.*

Harald Wiberg

Children are playing in the cottage.

Soon they will be going to bed.

They don't know about the fox

and the Tomten out in the snow.

The fox sneaks around to the cowshed.

There must be something there for a hungry fox to eat.

*Creep silently, Reynard, so that no one will hear you!*

Now everything is quiet.

The cows are fast asleep.

What do cows care about a fox?

But the cowshed mice are awake.


"Come on, Reynard, catch us if you can!
We have a hole in the floor. Ask the cat, she'll tell you.
Come on, come on, come on, Reynard,
come and catch us if you can!"

Who cares for mice? There are other things which taste better.

*Look out, hens, for Reynard is coming!*

"The fox is here! Oh, help, help!"

Then steps are heard outside.

The hens hear them and the fox hears them.

Who is coming through the snow?

Only an old, old tomten, who guards the farm at night.


*Were you frightened, Reynard?*
*Have you seen the Tomten before,*
*going his rounds from building to building?*

Harald Wilberg

An old tomten knows that a fox can be hungry.

"You know that no one
is allowed to steal our hens, don't you, Reynard?"

"Hens," says Reynard.
"Who thought of stealing hens?"

"Didn't you stick your hungry nose through that hole?

As long as I am on guard,

every hen can sit safely on her perch."

But an old tomten knows that a fox can be hungry.

"Here you are, eat this porridge!"

Every night the children fill the Tomten's bowl with porridge.
They have never seen him, but they know he is there.

"It's good, isn't it?

Eat, Reynard, you can share my porridge.

Every night if you like. But don't touch our hens!"


"We'll see," says the fox, "but thank you, anyway."

Harald Wiberg

Satisfied and happy,

Reynard goes, through the forest back to his den.

It is a night for foxes and tomtens.

People are fast asleep in their beds, but the morning star

has already risen above the edge of the forest.

Harald Wiberg